ILLUSTRATED CLASSICS

Rapunzel

AND OTHER CLASSIC TALES

COMPILED BY

PATRICIA MOORE

NEW DELHI (INDIA)

ILLUSTRATED CLASSICS

Rapunzel

AND OTHER CLASSIC TALES

Published by

MG BOOKS

An Imprint of

MAANU GRAPHICS

MAANU GRAPHICS

(PUBLISHERS OF GENERAL BOOKS)

5FF, Ganpati Bhawan, 21 Ansari Road,
Darya Ganj, New Delhi-110002
Ph: 65285220, 64138266
E-mail : maanugraphics@yahoo.com
mgbooks.maanu@yahoo.com

Printed at :
Satyam Enterprises, Delhi

CONTENTS

The Most Lovely Garden

RAPUNZEL

Once upon a time there lived a man and his wife who had no children. These good people had a little window at the back of their house, which looked into the most lovely garden, full of all manner of beautiful flowers and vegetables; but the garden was surrounded by a high wall, and no one dared to enter it, for it belonged to a witch of great power, who was feared by the whole world.

One day the woman stood at the window overlooking the garden, and saw there a bed full of the finest turnips: the leaves looked so fresh and green that she longed to eat them. Her desire grew day by day, and just because she knew she couldn't possibly get any, she pined away and became quite pale and wretched. Then her husband grew alarmed and said:

"How Dare You?"

"What ails you, dear wife?"

"Oh," she answered, "if I don't get some turnips to eat out of the garden behind the house, I know [shall die."

The man, who loved her dearly, thought to himself, "Come!

Rather than let your wife die you shall fetch her some turnips, no matter the cost." So at dusk he climbed over the wall into the witch's garden, and, hastily gathering a handful of turnip leaves, he returned with them to his wife.

She made them into a salad, which tasted so good that her longing for the forbidden food was greater than ever. If she were to know any peace of mind, there was nothing for it but that her husband should climb over the garden wall again, and fetch her some more. So at dusk over the wall he went, but when he reached the other side he drew back in terror, for there, standing before him, was the old witch.

"How dare you," she said, with a wrathful glance, "climb into my garden and steal my turnips like a common thief? You shall suffer for your foolhardiness."

"Rapunzel, Rapunzel, Let Down Your Hair"

"Oh!" he implored, "pardon my presumption; necessity alone drove me to the deed. My wife saw your turnips from her window, and conceived such a desire that she would certainly have died if her wish had not been gratified."

Then the witch's anger was a little appeased, and she said: "If it's as you say, you may take as many turnips away with you as you like, but on one condition – that you give me the child your wife will shortly bring into the world. All shall go well with it, and I will look after it like a mother."

The man in his terror agreed to everything she asked, and as soon as the child was born the witch appeared, and having given it the name of Rapunzel, she carried it off with her.

Rapunzel was the most beautiful child under the sun. When she was twelve years old the witch shut her up in a tower in the middle of a great wood, which had neither stairs nor doors, only high up at the very top a small window. When the old witch wanted to get in she stood underneath and called out:

"Rapunzel, Rapunzel,
Let down your hair,"

for Rapunzel had wonderful long hair, and it was as fine as spun gold. Whenever she heard the witch's voice she unloosed her braids, and let her hair fall down out of the window about twenty yards below, and the old witch climbed up by it.

After they had lived like this for a few years, it happened one day that a Prince was riding through the wood and passed by the tower. As he drew near it he heard someone singing so sweetly that he stood spell-bound and listened. It was Rapunzel in her loneliness trying to while away the time by letting her sweet voice ring out into the wood.

The Prince longed to see the owner of the voice, but he sought in vain for a door in the tower. He rode home, but he was so haunted by the song he had heard that he returned every day to the wood and listened.

One day, when he was standing thus behind a tree, he saw the old witch approach and heard her call out: "Rapunzel, Rapunzel, Let down your hair."

Then Rapunzel let down her braids, and the witch climbed up by them.

"So that's the staircase, is it?" said the Prince. "Then I too will climb it and try my luck."

On the following day at dusk, he went to the foot of the tower and cried:

"Rapunzel, Rapunzel,
Let down your hair,"

and as soon as she had let it down the Prince climbed up.

At first Rapunzel was terribly frightened when a man came in, for she had never seen one before; but the Prince spoke to her so kindly, and told her at once that his heart had been so touched by her singing, that he felt he should know no peace of mind till he had seen her.

Very soon Rapunzel forgot her fear, and when he asked her to marry him she consented at once. "For," she thought, "he is young and handsome, and I will certainly be happier with him than with the old witch."

So she put her hand in his and said:

"Yes, I will gladly go with you, only how am I to get down out of the tower? Every time

"Then I Too Will Climb It"

you come to see me you must bring a skein of silk with you, and I will make a ladder of them, and when it is finished I will climb down by it, and you will take me away on your horse."

They arranged that, till the ladder was ready, he was to come to her every evening, because the old woman was with her during the day.

The old witch, of course, knew nothing of what was going on, till one day Rapunzel, not thinking of what she was about, turned to the witch and said: "How is it, good mother, that you are so much harder to pull up than the young Prince? He is always with me in a moment."

"Oh! You wicked child," cried the witch. "What is this I hear? I thought I had hidden you safely from the whole world, and in spite of it you have managed to deceive me!"

In her wrath she seized Rapunzel's beautiful hair, wound it round and round her left hand, and then grasping a pair of scissors in her right, snip snap, off it came, and the beautiful braids lay on the ground. And, worse than this, she was so hard-hearted that

"What Is This I Hear?"

she took Rapunzel to a lonely desert place, and there left her to live in loneliness and misery.

But on the evening of the day in which she had driven poor Rapunzel away, the witch fastened the braids on to a hook in the window, and when the Prince came and called out:

> "Rapunzel, Rapunzel,
> Let down your hair,"

she let them down, and the Prince climbed up as usual, but instead of his beloved Rapunzel he found the old witch, who fixed her evil, glittering eyes on him, and cried mockingly:

"Ah, ah! You thought to find your lady love, but the pretty bird has flown and its song is dumb; the cat caught it, and will scratch out your eyes, too. Rapunzel is lost to you forever – you will never see her again."

The Prince was beside himself with grief, and in his despair he jumped right down from the tower, and, though he escaped with his life, the thorns among which he fell pierced his eyes. Then he wandered through the

Then He Led Her To His Kingdom

wood, blind and miserable, eating nothing but roots and berries, and weeping and lamenting the loss of his lovely bride. So he wandered about for some years, as wretched and unhappy as he could be, when at last he came to the desert place where Rapunzel was living.

Of a sudden he heard a voice which seemed strangely familiar to him. He walked eagerly in the direction of the sound, and when he was quite close, Rapunzel recognized him and fell on his neck and wept.

Two of her tears touched his eyes, and in a moment they became quite clear again, and he saw as well as he had ever done. Then he led her to his kingdom, where they were received and welcomed with great joy, and they lived happily ever after.

He Rode Into Town

THE FISH AND THE RING

Once upon a time, there was a mighty baron who was a great magician and knew everything that would come to pass. One day, when his little boy was four years old, he looked into the Book of Fate to see what would happen to him.

To his dismay, he found that his son would wed a lowly maid that had just been born in a house under the shadow of the nearby minster.

Now the Baron knew the father of the little girl was very, very poor, and he had five children already. So he called for his horse, and rode into town and passed by the other's house, and saw him sitting by the door, sad and doleful.

He dismounted and went up to him and

She Floated Till Cast Ashore

said: "What is the matter, my good man?"

And the man said: "Well, your honor, the fact is, I've five children already, and now a sixth's come, a little lass, and where to get the bread from to fill their mouths, that's more than I can say."

"Don't be downhearted, my man," said the Baron. "If that's your trouble, I can help you. I'll take away the last little one, and you won't have to bother about her."

"Thank you kindly, sir," said the man; and he went in and brought out the lass and gave her to the Baron, who mounted his horse and rode away with her. And when he got by the bank of the river, he threw the little thing into the river, and rode off to his castle.

But the little lass didn't sink; her clothes kept her up for a time, and she floated, and she floated, till she was cast ashore just in front of a fisherman's hut. There the fisherman found her, and took pity on the poor little thing and took her into his house, and she lived there till she was fifteen years old, and a fine handsome girl.

"Yours Affectionately, Humphrey"

One day it happened that the Baron went out hunting with some companions along the banks of the river, and stopped at the fisherman's hut to get a drink and the girl came out to give it to them. They all noticed her beauty, and one of them said to the Baron: "You can read fates, Baron, whom will she marry, d'ye think ?"

"Oh! that's easy to guess," said the Baron, "some yokel or other. But I'll cast her horoscope. Come here, girl, and tell me on what day you were born."

"I don't know, sir," said the girl, "I was picked up just here after having been brought down by the river about fifteen years ago."

Then the Baron knew who she was, and when they went away, he rode back and said to the girl: "Hark ye, girl, I will make your fortune. Take this letter to my brother, and you will be settled for life." The girl took the letter and said she would go. Now this was what he had written in the letter:

"DEAR BROTHER – Take the bearer and put her to death immediately.

"Yours affectionately,
HUMPHREY."

"Till You Can Show Me That Ring"

Soon after the girl set out and slept for the night at a little inn. Now that very night a band of robbers broke into the inn, and searched the girl, who had no money, but only the letter. So they opened this and read it, and thought it a shame.

The captain of the robbers took a pen and paper and wrote this letter:

"DEAR BROTHER – Take the bearer and marry her to my son immediately.

"Yours affectionately,
HUMPHREY."

And then he gave it to the girl, bidding her begone. So she went on to the Baron's brother, a noble knight, with whom the Baron's son was staying. When she gave the letter to the brother, he gave orders for the wedding to be prepared at once, and they were married that very day.

Soon after, the Baron himself came to his brother's castle, and what was his surprise to find that the very thing he had plotted against had come to pass! But he was not to be put off that way; and he took the girl for a walk, as he said, along the cliffs. And when he got her

"Send the Cook Who Cooked That Fish"

all alone, he took her by the arms, and was going to throw her over.

But she begged hard for her life. "I have not done anything," she said, "if only you will spare me, I will do whatever you wish. I will never see you or your son again till you desire it."

Then the Baron took off his gold ring and threw it into the sea, saying: "Never let me see your face till you can show me that ring," and he let her go.

The poor girl wandered on and on, till at last she came to a great noble's castle, and she asked to have some work given to her; and they made her the scullion girl of the castle, for she had been used to such work in the fisherman's hut.

Now one day, who should she see coming up to the noble's house but the Baron, his brother, and his son, her husband. She didn't know what to do, but thought they would not see her in the castle kitchen.

So she went back to her work with a sigh, and set to cleaning a huge big fish that was to be boiled for their dinner.

And, as she was cleaning it, she saw something shine inside it, and what do you think she found? Why, there was the Baron's ring, the very one he had thrown over the cliff!

She was glad indeed to see it, you may be sure. Then she cooked the fish as nicely as she could, and served it up.

Well, when the fish came on the table, the guests liked it so well that they asked the noble who cooked it.

He said he didn't know, but called to his servants: "Ho, there, send the cook who cooked that fine fish." So they went down to the kitchen and told the girl she was wanted in the hall. Then she made herself ready and put the Baron's gold ring on her thumb and went up into the hall.

When the banqueters saw such a young and beautiful cook they were surprised. But the Baron was in a tower of a temper, and started up as if he would do her some violence.

The girl went up to him with her hand before her with the ring on it, and she put it down before him on the table.

Then at last the Baron saw that no one could fight against Fate, and he handed her to a seat and announced to all the company that this was his son's true wife.

He took her and his son home to his castle, and they all lived as happy as could be ever afterwards.

A Ship to Float on Both Land and Sea

HOW THE HERMIT HELPED WIN THE PRINCESS

Long ago there lived a very rich man who had three sons. When he felt himself to be dying he divided his property amongst them, making them share alike, both in money and lands. Soon after he died the King set forth a proclamation through the whole country that whoever could build a ship that should float both on land and sea should have his daughter to wife.

The eldest brother, when he heard it, said to the others, "I think I will spend some of my money in trying to build that ship, as I should like to have the King for my father-in-law."

Driven Away, Like the Rest

So he called together all the shipbuilders in the land, and gave them orders to begin the ship without delay. Trees were cut down, and great preparations made, and in a few days everybody knew what it was all for; and there was a crowd of old people pressing round the gates of the yard, where the young man spent the most of his day.

"Ah, master, give us work," they said, "so that we may earn our bread."

But he only gave them hard words, and spoke roughly to them. "You are old, and have lost your strength; of what use are you?" And he drove them away. Then came some boys and prayed him, "Master, give us work," but he answered them, "Of what use can you be, weaklings as you are! Get you gone!" And if any presented themselves that were not skilled workmen he would have none of them.

At last there knocked at the gate a little old man with a long white beard who said, "Will you give me work, so that I may earn my bread?" But he was only driven away like the rest.

"I Am Not Rich Enough"

The ship took a long while to build, and cost a great deal of money, and when it was launched a sudden squall rose, and it fell to pieces, and with it all the young man's hopes of winning the Princess. By this time he had not a penny left, so he went back to his two brothers and told his tale.

And the second brother said to himself as he listened, "Certainly he has managed very badly, but I should like to see if I can't do better, and win the Princess for my own self." So he called together all the shipbuilders throughout the country, and gave them orders to build a ship which should float on the land as well as on the sea.

But his heart was no softer than his brother's, and every man who was not a skilled workman was chased away with hard words. Last came the white-bearded man, but he fared no better than the rest.

When the ship was finished the launch took place, and everything seemed going smoothly when a gale sprang up, and the vessel was dashed to pieces on the rocks. The young man had spent his whole fortune on it, and now it was all swallowed up, he was forced to beg

"I Am Putting the Fog Into My Sack"

shelter from his youngest brother.

When he told his story the youngest said to himself, "I am not rich enough to support us all three. I had better take my turn, and if I manage to win the Princess there will be her fortune as well as my own for us to live on."

So he called together all the shipbuilders in the kingdom, and gave orders that a new ship should be built. Then all the old people came and asked for work, and he answered cheerfully, "Oh, yes, there is plenty for everybody;" and when the boys begged to be allowed to help he found something that they could do.

And when the old man with the long white beard stood before him, praying that he might earn his bread, he replied, "Oh, father, I could not suffer you to work, but you shall be overseer, and look after the rest."

Now the old man was a holy hermit, and when he saw how kind-hearted the youth was, he determined to do all he could for him to gain the wish of his heart.

By and by, when the ship was finished, the hermit said to his young friend, "Now you can go and claim the King's daughter, for the ship will float both by land and sea."

"Oh, good father," cried the young man, "you will not forsake me? Stay with me, I pray you, and lead me to the King!"

"If you wish it, I will," said the hermit, "on condition that you will give me half of anything you get."

"Oh, if that is all," answered he, "it is easily promised!" And they set out together on the ship.

After they had gone some distance they saw a man standing in a thick fog, which he was trying to put into a sack.

"Oh, good father," exclaimed the youth, "what can he be doing?"

"Ask him," said the old man.

"What are you doing, my fine fellow?"

"I am putting the fog into my sack. That is my business."

"Ask him if he will come with us," whispered the hermit.

And the man answered: "If you will give

me enough to eat and drink I will gladly stay with you."

So they took him on their ship, and the youth said, as they started off again, "Good father, before we were two, and now we are three!"

After they had travelled a little further they met a man who had torn up half the forest, and was carrying all the trees on his shoulders.

"Good father," exclaimed the youth, "only look! What can he have done that for?"

"Ask him why he has torn up all those trees."

And the man replied, "Why, I've merely been gathering a handful of brushwood."

"Beg him to come with us," whispered the hermit.

And the strong man answered, "Willingly, as long as you give me enough to eat and drink." And he came on the ship.

And the youth said to the hermit, "Good father, before we were three, and now we are four."

"A Handful of Brushwood"

The ship travelled on again, and some miles further on they saw a man drinking out of a stream till he had nearly drunk it dry.

"Good father," said the youth, "just look at that man! Did you ever see anybody drink like that?"

"Ask him why he does it," answered the hermit.

"Why, there is nothing very odd in taking a mouthful of water!" replied the man, standing up.

"Beg him to come with us." And the youth did so.

"With pleasure, as long as you give me enough to eat and drink."

And the youth whispered to the hermit, "Good father, before we were four, and now we are five."

A little way along they noticed another man in the middle of a stream, who was shooting into the water.

"Good father," said the youth, "what can he be shooting at?"

"I Hit Everything I Aim At"

"Ask him," answered the hermit.

"Hush, hush!" cried the man. "Now you have frightened it away. In the Underworld sits a quail on a tree, and I wanted to shoot it. That is my business. I hit everything I aim at."

"Ask him if he will come with us."

And the man replied, "With all my heart, as long as I get enough to eat and drink."

So they took him into the ship, and the young man whispered, "Good father, before we were five, and now we are six."

Off they went again, and before they had gone far they met a man striding towards them whose steps were so long that while one foot was on the north of the island the other was right down in the south.

"Good father, look at him! What long steps he takes!"

"Ask him why he does it," replied the hermit.

"Oh, I am only going out for a little walk," answered he.

"It Is Not Enough"

"Ask him if he will come with us."

"Gladly, if you will give me as much as I want to eat and drink," said he, climbing up into the ship.

And the young man whispered, "Good father, before we were six, and now we are seven." But the hermit knew what he was doing, and why he gathered these strange people into the ship.

After many days, at last they reached the town where lived the King and his daughter. They stopped the vessel right in front of the palace, and the young man went in and bowed low before the king.

"O Majesty, I have done your bidding, and now is the ship built that can travel over land and sea. Give me my regard, and Ice me have your daughter to wife."

But the King said to himself, "What! Am I to wed my daughter to a man of whom I know nothing? Not even whether he be rich or poor — a knight or a beggar."

And aloud he spoke: "It is not enough that you have managed to build the ship. You must find a runner who shall take this letter to the ruler of the Underworld, and bring me the answer back in an hour."

"That is not in the bond," answered the young man.

"Well, do as you like," replied the King, "only you will not get my daughter."

The young man went out, sorely troubled, to tell his old friend what had happened.

"Silly boy!" cried the hermit. "Accept his terms at once. And send off the long-legged man with the letter. He will take it in no time at all."

So the youth's heart leapt for joy, and he returned to the King. "Majesty, I accept your terms. Here is the messenger who will do what you wish."

The King had no choice but to give the man the letter, and he strode off, making short work of the distance that lay between the palace and the Underworld.

He soon found the ruler, who looked at the letter, and said to him, "Wait a little while I write the answer;" but the man was so tired with his quick walk that he went sound asleep, and forgot all about his errand.

All this time the youth was anxiously counting the minutes till he could get back, and stood with his eyes fixed on the road down which his messenger must come.

"What can be keeping him?" he said to the hermit when the hour was nearly up.

Then the hermit sent for the man who could hit every thing he aimed at, and said to him, "Just see why the messenger stays so long."

"Oh, he is sound asleep in the palace of the Underworld. However, I can soon wake him." Then he drew his bow, and shot an arrow straight into the man's knee. The messenger awoke with a start, and when he saw that the hour had almost run out he snatched up the answer and rushed back with such speed that the clock had not yet struck when he entered the palace.

Now the young man thought he was sure of his bride, but the King said, "Still you have not done enough. Before I give you my daughter you must find a man who can drink half the contents of my cellar in one day."

"I Can Soon Wake Him"

"That is not in the bond," complained the poor youth.

"Well, do as you like, only you will not get my daughter."

The young man went sadly out, and asked the hermit what he was to do.

"Silly boy!" said he. "Why, tell the man to do it who drinks up everything."

So they sent for the man and said, "Do you think you are able to drink half the royal cellar in one day?"

"Dear me, yes, and as much more as you want," answered he. "I am never satisfied."

The King was not pleased at the young man agreeing so readily, but he had no choice, and ordered the servant to be taken downstairs. Oh, how he enjoyed himself! All day long he drank, and drank, and drank, till, instead of half the cellar, he had drunk the whole, and there was not a cask but what stood empty.

When the King saw this he said to the youth, "You have conquered, and I can no longer withhold my daughter. But, as her

"Drink Half the Royal Cellar in One Day"

dowry, I shall only give so much as one man can carry away."

"But," answered he, "let a man be ever so strong, he cannot carry more than a hundredweight, and what is that for a King's daughter?"

"Well, do as you like; I have said my say. It is your affair – not mine."

The young man was puzzled, and did not know what to reply, for, though he would gladly have married the Princess without a sixpence, he had spent all his money in building the ship, and knew he could not give her all she wanted.

So he went to the hermit and said to him, "The King will only give for her dowry as much as a man can carry. I have no money of my own left, and my brothers have none either."

"Silly boy! Why, you have only got to fetch the man who carried half the forest on his shoulders."

And the youth was glad, and called the strong man, and told him what he must do.

He Piled All on His Back

"Take everything you can, till you are bent double. Never mind if you leave the palace bare."

The strong man promised, and nobly kept his word. He piled all he could see on his back – chairs, tables, wardrobes, chests of gold and silver – till there was nothing left to pile. At last he took the King's crown, and put it on the top. He carried his burden to the ship and stowed his treasures away, and the youth followed, leading the King's daughter.

But the King was left raging in his empty palace, and he called together his army, and got ready his ships of war, in order that he might go after the vessel and bring back what had been taken away.

And the King's ships sailed very fast, and soon caught up with the little vessel, and the sailors all shouted for joy. Then the hermit looked out and saw how near they were, and he said to the youth, "Do you see that?"

The youth shrieked and cried, "Ah, good father, it is a fleet of ships, and they are chasing us, and in a few moments they will be upon us!"

But the hermit bade him call the man who had the fog in his sack, and the sack was opened and the fog flew out, and hung right round the King's ships, so that they could see nothing. So they sailed back to the palace, and told the King what strange things had happened. Meanwhile the young man's vessel reached home in safety.

"Well, here you are once more," said the hermit; "and now you can fulfill the promise you made me to give me the half of all you had."

"That will I do with all my heart," answered the youth, and began to divide all his treasures, putting part on one side for himself and setting aside the other for his friend. "Good father, it is finished," said he at length; "there is nothing more left to divide."

"Nothing more left!" cried the hermit. "Why, you have forgotten the best thing of all!"

"What can that be?" asked he. "We have divided everything,"

"And the King's daughter?" said the hermit.

Then the young man's heart stood still, for he loved her dearly. But he answered, "It is well; I have sworn, and I will keep my word," and drew his sword to cut her in pieces.

When the hermit saw that he held his honor dearer than his wife, he lifted his hand and cried "Hold! She is yours, and all the treasures too. I gave you my help because you had pity on those that were in need. And when you are in need yourself, call upon me, and I will come to you."

As he spoke, he softly touched their heads and vanished.

The next day the wedding took place, and the two brothers came to the house, and they all lived happily together, but they never forgot the holy man who had been such a good friend.

From the Four Corners of the World

PRINCESS MAYBLOSSOM

Once upon a time there lived a King and Queen whose children had all died, first one and then another, until at last only one little daughter remained, and the Queen was at her wits' end to know where to find a really good nurse who would take care of her, and bring her up.

A herald was sent who blew a trumpet at every street corner, and commanded all the best nurses to appear before the Queen, that she might choose one for the little Princess.

So on the appointed day the whole palace was crowded with nurses, who came from the four corners of the world to offer themselves, until the Queen declared that if she was ever to see the half of them, they must be brought out to her, one by one, as she sat in a shady wood near the palace.

She Hid Herself in a Hollow Tree

This was accordingly done, and the nurses, after they had made their curtsey to the King and Queen, ranged themselves in a line before her that she might choose. Most of them were fair and fat and charming, but there was one who was ugly, and spoke a strange language which nobody could understand.

The Queen wondered how she dared offer herself, and she was told to go away, as she certainly would not do. Upon which she muttered something and passed on, but hid herself in a hollow tree, from which she could see all that happened.

The Queen, without giving her another thought, chose a pretty rose-faced nurse, but no sooner was her choice made than a snake, which was hidden in the grass, bit that very nurse on her foot, so that she fell down as if dead.

The Queen was very much vexed by this accident, but she soon selected another, who was just stepping forward when an eagle flew by and dropped a large tortoise upon her head, which was cracked in pieces like an egg shell.

Whirled Through the Air

At this the Queen was much horrified; nevertheless, she chose a third time, but with no better fortune, for the nurse, moving quickly, ran into the branch of a tree and blinded herself with a thorn.

Then the Queen in dismay cried that there must be some malignant influence at work, and that she would choose no more that day; and she had just risen to return to the palace when she heard peals of malicious laughter behind her, and turning round saw the ugly stranger whom she had dismissed, who was making very merry over the disasters and mocking everyone, but especially the Queen.

This annoyed Her Majesty very much, and she was about to order that she should be arrested, when the witch – for she was a witch – with two blows from a wand summoned a chariot of fire drawn by winged dragons, and was whirled off through the air uttering threats and cries.

When the King saw this he cried:

"Alas! Now we are ruined indeed, for that was no other than the Fairy Carabosse, who has had a grudge against me ever since I was a boy and put sulphur into her porridge one day for fun."

Then the Queen began to cry.

"If I had only known who it was," she said, "I would have done my best to make friends with her; now I suppose all is lost."

The King was sorry to have frightened her so much, and proposed that they should go and hold a council as to what was best to be done to avert the misfortunes which Carabosse certainly meant to bring upon the little Princess.

So all the counsellors were summoned to the palace, and when they had shut every door and window, and stuffed up every keyhole that they might not be overheard, they talked the affair over, and decided that every fairy for a thousand leagues round should be invited to the christening of the Princess, and that the time of the ceremony should be kept a profound secret, in case the Fairy Carabosse should take it into her head to attend it.

The Queen and her ladies set to work to prepare presents for the fairies who were invited: for each one a blue velvet cloak, a petticoat of apricot satin, a pair of high-heeled shoes, some sharp needles, and a pair of golden scissors.

Of all the fairies the Queen knew, only five were able to come on the day appointed, but they began immediately to bestow gifts upon the Princess.

One promised that she should be perfectly beautiful, the second that she should understand anything – no matter what – the first time it was explained to her, the third that she should sing like a nightingale, the fourth that she should succeed in everything she undertook, and the fifth was opening her mouth to speak when a tremendous rumbling was heard in the chimney, and Carabosse, all covered with soot, came rolling down, crying:

"I say that she shall be the unluckiest of the unlucky until she is twenty years old."

Then the Queen and all the fairies began to beg and beseech her to think better of it, and not be so unkind to the poor little Princess, who had never done her any harm. But the ugly old Fairy only grunted and made no answer. So the last Fairy, who had not yet

"Unlunkiest of the Unlucky"

given her gift, tried to mend matters by promising the Princess a long and happy life after the fatal time was over.

At this Carabosse laughed maliciously, and climbed away up the chimney, leaving them all in great consternation, especially the Queen. However, she entertained the fairies splendidly, and gave them beautiful ribbons, of which they are very fond, in addition to the other presents.

When they were going away the oldest Fairy said that they were of opinion that it would be best to shut the Princess up in some place, with her waiting-women, so that she might not see anyone else until she was twenty years old.

So the King had a tower built for that purpose. It had no windows, so it was lighted with wax candles, and the only way into it was by an underground passage, which had iron doors only twenty feet apart, and guards were posted everywhere.

The Princess had been named Mayblossom, because she was as fresh and blooming as Spring itself, and she grew up tall and beautiful, and everything she did and

The King Had a Tower Built

said was charming. Every time the King and Queen came to see her they were more delighted with her than before, but though she was weary of the tower, and often begged them to take her away from it, they always refused. The Princess's nurse, who had never left her, sometimes told her about the world outside the tower, and though the Princess had never seen anything for herself, yet she always understood exactly, thanks to the second Fairy's gift.

Often the King said to the Queen:

"We were cleverer than Carabosse after all. Our Mayblossom will be happy in spite of her predictions."

And the Queen laughed until she was tired, at the idea of having outwitted the old Fairy. They had caused the Princess's portrait to be painted and sent to all the neighboring courts, for in four days she would have completed her twentieth year, and it was time to decide whom she should marry.

All the town was rejoicing at the thought of the Princess's approaching freedom, and when the news came that King Merlin was sending his ambassador to ask her in

The Princess Was Wild to See the Procession

marriage for his son, they were still more delighted.

The nurse, who kept the Princess informed of everything that went forward in the town, did not fail to repeat the news that so closely concerned her, and gave such a description of the splendor in which the ambassador Fanfaronade would enter the town, that the Princess was wild to see the procession for herself.

"What an unhappy creature I am," she cried, "to be shut up in this dismal tower as if I had committed some crime! I have never seen the sun, or the stars, or a horse, or a monkey, or a lion, except in pictures, and though the King and Queen tell me I am to be set free when I am twenty, I believe they only say it to keep me amused when they never mean to let me out at all."

And then she began to cry, and her nurse, and the nurse's daughter, and the cradle-rocker, and the nursery-maid, who all loved her dearly, cried too for company, so that nothing could be heard but sobs and sighs. It was a scene of woe.

When the Princess saw that they all pitied

Fanfaronade Himself Upon a White Horse

her she made up her mind to have her own way. So she declared that she would starve herself to death if they did not find some means of letting her see Fanfaronade's grand entry into the town.

"If you really love me," she said, "you will manage it, somehow or other, and the King and Queen need never know anything about it."

Then the nurse and all the others cried harder than ever, and said everything they could think of to turn the Princess from her idea. But the more they said the more determined she was, and at last they consented to make a tiny hole in the tower on the side that looked towards the city gates.

After scratching and scraping all day and all night, they presently made a hole through which they could, with great difficulty, push a very slender needle, and out of this the Princess looked at the daylight for the first time. She was so dazzled and delighted by what she saw, that there she stayed, never taking her eyes away from the peep-hole for a single minute, until presently the ambassador's procession appeared in sight.

At the head of it rode Fanfaronade himself upon a white horse, which pranced and caracoled to the sound of the trumpets. Nothing could have been more splendid than the ambassador's attire. His coat was nearly hidden under an embroidery of pearls and diamonds, his boots were solid gold, and from his helmet floated scarlet plumes. At the sight of him the Princess lost her wits entirely, and determined that Fanfaronade and nobody else would she marry.

"It is quite impossible," she said, "that his master should be half as handsome and delightful. I am not ambitious, and having spent all my life in this tedious tower, anything – even a house in the country – will seem a delightful change. I am sure that bread and water shared with Fanfaronade will please me far better than roast chicken and sweetmeats with anybody else."

And so she went on talk, talk, talking, until her waiting-women wondered where she got it all from. But when they tried to stop her, and suggested that her high rank made it perfectly impossible that she should do any such thing, she would not listen, and ordered them to be silent.

As soon as the ambassador arrived at the palace, the Queen started to fetch her daughter.

All the streets were spread with carpets, and the windows were full of ladies who were waiting to see the Princess, and carried baskets of flowers and sweetmeats to shower upon her as she passed.

They had hardly begun to get the Princess ready when a dwarf arrived, mounted upon an elephant. He came from the five fairies, and brought for the Princess a crown, a scepter, and a robe of golden brocade, with a petticoat marvelously embroidered with butterflies' wings. They also sent a casket of jewels, so splendid that no one had ever seen anything like it before, and the Queen was perfectly dazzled when she opened it.

But the Princess scarcely gave a glance to any of these treasures, for she thought of nothing but Fanfaronade. The Dwarf was rewarded with a gold piece, and decorated with so many ribbons that it was hardly possible to see him at all.

The Princess sent to each of the fairies a new spinning-wheel with a distaff of cedar

A Huge Owl Skimmed Up to the Princess

wood, and the Queen said she must look through her treasures and find something very charming to send them also.

When the Princess was arrayed in all the gorgeous things the Dwarf had brought, she was more beautiful than ever, and as she walked along the streets the people cried: "How pretty she is! How pretty she is!"

The procession consisted of the Queen, the Princess, five dozen other Princesses, her cousins; and ten dozen who came from the neighboring kingdoms; and as they proceeded at a stately pace the sky began to grow dark, then suddenly the thunder growled, and rain and hail fell in torrents.

The Queen put her royal mantle over her head, and all the Princesses did the same with their trains. Mayblossom was just about to follow their example when a terrific croaking, as of an immense army of crows, rooks, ravens, screech-owls, and all birds of ill-omen was heard, and at the same instant a huge owl skimmed up to the Princess, and threw over her a scarf woven of spiders' webs and embroidered with bats' wings.

The Ambassador Appeared Before Her

And then peals of mocking laughter rang through the air, and they knew that this was another of the Fairy Carabosse's unpleasant jokes.

The Queen was terrified at such an evil omen, and tried to pull the black scarf from the Princess's shoulders, but it really seemed as if it must be nailed on, it clung so closely.

"Ah!" cried the Queen, "Can nothing appease this enemy of ours? What good was it that I sent her more than fifty pounds of sweetmeats, and as much again of the best sugar, not to mention two hams? She is as angry as ever."

While she lamented in this way, and everybody was as wet as if they had been dragged through a river, the Princess still thought of nothing but the ambassador, and just at this moment he appeared before her, with the King, and there was a great blowing of trumpets, and all the people shouted louder than ever.

Fanfaronade was not generally at a loss for something to say, but when he saw the Princess, she was so much more beautiful and majestic than he had expected that he could

"You Came to Speak for Another"

only stammer out a few words, and entirely forgot the harangue which he had been learning for months, and knew well enough to have repeated it in his sleep.

To gain time to remember at least part of it, he made several low bows to the Princess, who on her side dropped half-a-dozen curtseys without stopping to think, and then she said, to relieve his evident embarrassment:

"Sir Ambassador, I am sure that everything you intend to say is charming, since it is you who mean to say it; but let us make haste into the palace, as it is pouring cats and dogs, and the wicked Fairy Carabosse will be amused to see us all stand dripping here. When we are once under shelter we can laugh at her."

Upon this the ambassador found his tongue, and replied gallantly that the Fairy had evidently foreseen the flames that would be kindled by the bright eyes of the Princess, and had sent this deluge to extinguish them.

Then he offered his hand to conduct the Princess, and she said softly: "As you could not possibly guess how much I like you, Sir

She Took the King's Dagger and They Ran Out Together

Fanfaronade, I am obliged to tell you plainly that, since I saw you enter the town on your beautiful prancing horse, I have been sorry that you came to speak for another instead of for yourself. So, if you feel as I do, I will marry you instead of your master. Of course I know you are not a Prince, but I shall be just as fond of you as if you were, and we can go and live in some cozy little corner of the world, and be as happy as the days are long."

The ambassador thought he must be dreaming, and could hardly believe what the lovely Princess had said. He dared not answer, but only squeezed the Princess's hand until he really hurt her little finger, but she did not cry out.

When they reached the palace the King kissed his daughter on both cheeks, and said: "My little lambkin, are you willing to marry the great King Merlin's son, as this ambassador has come on his behalf to fetch you?"

"If you please, sire," said the Princess, dropping a curtsey.

"I consent also," said the Queen; "so let the banquet be prepared."

This was done with all speed, and everybody feasted except Mayblossom and Fanfaronade, who looked at one another and forgot everything else.

After the banquet came a ball, and after that a ballet, and at last they were all so tired that everyone feel asleep just where he sat. Only the lovers were as wide awake as mice, and the Princess, seeing that there was nothing to fear, said to Fanfaronade:

"Let us be quick and run away, for we shall never have a better chance than this."

Then she took the King's dagger, which was in a diamond sheath, and the Queen's neck-handkerchief, and gave her hand to Fanfaronade, who carried a lantern, and they ran out together into the muddy street and down to the seashore.

Here they got into a little boat in which the poor old boatman was sleeping, and when he woke up and saw the lovely Princess, with all her diamonds and her spiders'-web scarf, he did not know what to think, and obeyed her instantly when she commanded him to set out.

They could see neither moon nor stars, but in the Queen's neck-handkerchief there was a carbuncle which glowed like fifty torches.

Fanfaronade asked the Princess where she would like to go, but she only answered that she did not care where she went as long as he was with her.

"But, Princess," said he, "I dare not take you back to King Merlin's court. He would think hanging too good for me."

"Oh, in that case," she answered, "we had better go to Squirrel Island; it is lonely enough, and too far for anyone to follow us there."

So she ordered the old boatman to steer for Squirrel Island.

Meanwhile the day was breaking, and the King and Queen and all the courtiers began to wake up and rub their eyes, and think it was time to finish the preparations for the wedding. And the Queen asked for her neck-handkerchief, that she might look richly dressed for her daughter's ceremony.

Then there was a scurrying hither and thither, and a hunting everywhere: they

The Handkerchief Was Nowhere to Be Found

looked into every place, from the wardrobes to the stoves, and the Queen herself ran about from the garret to the cellar, but the handkerchief was nowhere to be found.

By this time the King had missed his dagger, and the search began all over again. They opened boxes and chests of which the keys had been lost for a hundred years, and found numbers of curious things, but not the dagger, and the King tore his beard, and the Queen tore her hair, for the handkerchief and the dagger were the most valuable things in the kingdom.

When the King saw that the search was hopeless he said:

"Never mind, let us make haste and get the wedding over before anything else is lost." And then he asked where the Princess was. Upon this her nurse came forward and said: "Sire, I have been seeking her these two hours, but she is nowhere to be found."

This was more than the Queen could bear. She gave a shriek of alarm and fainted away, and they had to pour two barrels of eau-de-cologne over her before she recovered.

Silence for Three Hours

When she came to herself everybody was looking for the Princess in the greatest terror and confusion, but as she did not appear, the King said to his page: "Go and find the Ambassador Fanfaronade, who is doubtless asleep in some corner, and tell him the sad news."

So the page hunted hither and thither, but Fanfaronade was no more to be found than the Princess, the dagger, or the neck-handkerchief!

Then the King summoned his counsellors and his guards, and, accompanied by the Queen, went into his great hall. As he had not had time to prepare his speech beforehand, the King ordered that silence should be kept for three hours, and at the end of that time he spoke as follows:

"Listen, great and small! My dear daughter Mayblossom is lost: whether she had been stolen away or has simply disappeared I cannot tell. The Queen's neck-handkerchief and my sword, which are worth their weight in gold, are also missing, and worst of all, the Ambassador Fanfaronade is nowhere to be found. I fear the King, his master, will come

The Nurse Came Forward

to seek him, and accuse us of having made mince-meat of him. I could bear even that if I had any money, but I assure you that the expenses of the wedding have completely ruined me. Advise me, then, my dear subjects, what had I better do to recover my daughter, Fanfaronade, and the other things."

This was the most eloquent speech the King had been known to make, and when everybody had done admiring it the Prime Minister made answer:

"Sire, we are all very sorry to see you so sorry. We would give everything we value in the world to take away the cause of your sorrow, but this seems to be another of the tricks of the Fairy Cara-bosse. The Princess's twenty unlucky years were not quite over, and really, if the truth must be told, I noticed that Fanfaronade and the Princess appeared to admire one another greatly. Perhaps this may give us some clue to the mystery of their disappearance."

Here the Queen interrupted him, saying, "Take care what you say, sir. Believe me, the Princess Mayblossom was far too well brought up to think of falling in love with an ambassador."

A Light Like a Great Fire

At this moment the nurse came forward, and, falling on her knees, confessed how they had made the little needle-hole in the tower, and how the Princess had declared when she saw the ambassador that she would marry him and nobody else.

Then the Queen was very angry, and gave the nurse, and the cradle-rocker, and the nursery-maid, such a scolding that they shook in their shoes.

But the Admiral Cocked-Hat interrupted her, crying: "Let us be off after this good-for-nothing Fanfaronade, for without a doubt he has run away with our Princess."

Then there was a great clapping of hands, and everybody shouted, "By all means let us be after him."

So while some embarked upon the sea, the others ran from kingdom to kingdom beating drums and blowing trumpets, and wherever a crowd collected they cried:

"Whoever wants a beautiful doll, sweetmeats of all kinds, a little pair of scissors, a golden robe, and a satin cap has only to say where Fanfaronade has hidden

The Old Boatman Told All He Knew

the Princess Mayblossom."

But the answer everywhere was, "You must go farther, we have not seen them."

However, those who went by sea were more fortunate, for after sailing about for some time they noticed a light before them which burned at night like a great fire. At first they dared not go near it, not knowing what it might be, but by-and-by it remained stationary over Squirrel Island, for, as you have guessed already, the light was the glowing of the carbuncle.

The Princess and Fanfaronade on landing upon the island had given the boatman a hundred gold pieces, and made him promise solemnly to tell no one where he had taken them; but the first thing that happened was that, as he rowed away, he got into the midst of the fleet, and before he could escape the Admiral had seen him and sent a boat after him.

When he was searched they found the gold pieces in his pocket, and as they were quite new coins, struck in honor of the Princess's wedding, the Admiral felt certain that the boatman must have been paid by the Princess

The Princess Ran Hither and Thither

to aid her in her flight. But he would not answer any questions, and pretended to be deaf and dumb.

Then the Admiral said: "Oh! Deaf and dumb is he? Lash him to the mast and give him a taste of the cat-o'-nine-tails. I don't know anything better than that for curing the deaf and dumb!"

And when the old boatman saw that he was in earnest, he told all he knew about the cavalier and the lady whom he had landed upon Squirrel Island, and the Admiral knew it must be the Princess and Fanfaronade; so he gave the order for the fleet to surround the island.

Meanwhile the Princess Mayblossom, who was by this time terribly sleepy, had found a grassy bank in the shade, and throwing herself down had already fallen asleep into a profound slumber, when Fanfaronade, who happened to be hungry and not sleepy, came and woke her up, saying very crossly:

"Pray, madam, how long do you mean to stay here? I see nothing to eat, and though you may be very charming, the sight of you does not prevent me from famishing."

"What! Fanfaronade," said the Princess, sitting up and rubbing her eyes, "is it possible that when I am here with you you can want anything else? You ought to be thinking all the time how happy you are."

"Happy!" cried he; "Say rather unhappy. I wish with all my heart that you were back in your dark tower again."

"Darling, don't be cross," said the Princess. "I will go and see if I can find some wild fruit for you."

"I wish you might find a wolf to eat you up," growled Fanfaronade.

The Princess, in great dismay, ran hither and thither all about the wood, tearing her dress, and hurting her pretty hands with the thorns and brambles, but she could find nothing to eat, and at last she had to go back sorrowfully to Fanfaronade.

When he saw that she came empty-handed he got up and left her, grumbling to himself.

The next day they searched again, but with no better success.

"Alas!" said the Princess, "If only I could

find something for you to eat, I should not mind being hungry myself."

"No, I should not mind that either," answered Fanfaronade.

"Is it possible," said she, "that you would not care if I died of hunger? Oh, Fanfaronade, you said you loved me!"

"That was when we were in quite another place and I was not hungry," said he. "It makes a great difference in one's ideas to be dying of hunger and thirst on a desert island."

At this the Princess was dreadfully vexed, and she sat down under a white rose bush and began to cry bitterly.

"Happy roses," she thought to herself, "they have only to blossom in the sunshine and be admired, and there is nobody to be unkind to them."

And the tears ran down her cheeks and splashed on to the rose-tree roots. Presently she was surprised to see the whole bush rustling and shaking, and a soft little voice from the prettiest rosebud said:

"Poor Princess! Look in the trunk of that

"Here Is a Honeycomb I Have Found"

tree, and you will find a honeycomb, but don't be foolish enough to share it with Fanfaronade."

Mayblossom ran to the tree, and sure enough there was the honey. Without losing a moment she ran with it to Fanfaronade, crying gaily:

"See, here is a honeycomb that I have found. I might have eaten it up all by myself, but I had rather share it with you."

But without looking at her or thanking her he snatched the honeycomb out of her hands and ate it all up – every bit, without offering her a morsel. Indeed, when she humbly asked for some he said mockingly that it was too sweet for her, and would spoil her teeth.

Mayblossom, more downcast than ever, went sadly away and sat down under an oak tree, and her tears and sighs were so piteous that the oak fanned her with his rustling leaves, and said:

"Take courage, pretty Princess, all is not lost yet. Take this pitcher of milk and drink it up, and whatever you do, don't leave a drop for Fanfaronade."

"You Cannot Be Thirsty"

The Princess, quite astonished, looked round, and saw a big pitcher full of milk, but before she could raise it to her lips the thought of how thirsty Fanfaronade must be, after eating at least fifteen pounds of honey, made her run back to him and say: "Here is a pitcher of milk; drink some, for you must be thirsty, I am sure; but pray save a little for me, as I am dying of hunger and thirst."

But he seized the pitcher and drank all it contained at a single draught, and then broke it to atoms on the nearest stone, saying, with a malicious smile: "As you have not eaten anything you cannot be thirsty."

"Ah!" cried the Princess, "I am well punished for disappointing the King and Queen, and running away with this ambassador, about whom I knew nothing."

And so saying she wandered away into the thickest part of the wood, and sat down under a thorn tree, where a nightingale was singing. Presently she heard him say: "Search under the bush, Princess; you will find some sugar, almonds, and some tarts there. But don't be silly enough to offer Fanfaronade any."

Every Preparation Was Made for War

And this time the Princess, who was fainting with hunger, took the nightingale's advice, and ate what she found all by herself. But Fanfaronade, seeing that she had found something good, and was not going to share it with him, ran after her in such a fury that she hastily drew out the Queen's carbuncle, which had the property of rendering people invisible if they were in danger, and when she was safely hidden from him she reproached him gently for his unkindness.

Meanwhile Admiral Cocked-Hat had despatched Jack-the-Chatterer-of-the-Straw-Boots, Courier in Ordinary to the Prime Minister, to tell the King that the Princess and the ambassador had landed on Squirrel Island, but that not knowing the country he had not pursued them, for fear of being captured by concealed enemies. Their Majesties were overjoyed at the news, and the King sent for a great book, each leaf of which was eight ells long. It was the work of a very clever Fairy, and contained a description of the whole earth. He very soon found that Squirrel Island was uninhabited.

"Go," said he to Jack-the-Chatterer, "tell the Admiral from me to land at once. I am surprised at his not having done so sooner." As soon as this message reached the fleet, every preparation was made for war, and the noise was so great that it reached the ears of the Princess, who at once flew to protect her ambassador. As he was not very brave he accepted her aid gladly.

"You stand behind me," said she, "and I will hold the carbuncle which will make us invisible, and with the King's dagger I can protect you from the enemy."

So when the soldiers landed they could see nothing, but the Princess touched them one after another with the dagger, and they fell insensible upon the sand, so that at last the Admiral, seeing that there was some enchantment, hastily gave orders for a retreat to be sounded, and got his men back into their boats in great confusion.

Fanfaronade, being once more left with the Princess, began to think that if he could get rid of her, and possess himself of the carbuncle and the dagger, he would be able to make his escape.

So as they walked back over the cliffs he gave the Princess a great push, hoping she would fall into the sea; but she stepped aside so quickly that he only succeeded in overbalancing himself, and over he went, and sank to the bottom of the sea like a lump of lead, and was never heard of any more.

While the Princess was still looking after him in horror, her attention was attracted by a rushing noise over her head, and looking up she saw two chariots approaching rapidly from opposite directions.

One was bright and glittering, and drawn by swans and peacocks, while the Fairy who sat in it was beautiful as a sunbeam; but the other was drawn by bats and ravens, and contained a frightful little Dwarf, who was dressed in a snake's skin, and wore a great toad upon her head for a hood.

The chariots met with a frightful crash in mid-air, and the Princess looked on in breathless anxiety while a furious battle took place between the lovely Fairy and her golden lance, and the hideous little Dwarf and her rusty pike. But very soon it was evident that the beauty had the best of it, and the Dwarf turned her bats' heads and flickered away in great confusion.

Two Chariots Approaching

The Fairy came down to where Mayblossom stood, and said, smiling: "You see, Princess, I have completely routed that malicious old Carabosse. Will you believe it! She actually wanted to claim authority over you forever, because you came out of the tower four days before the twenty years were ended. However, I think I have settled her pretensions, and I hope you will be very happy and enjoy the freedom I have won for you."

The Princess thanked her heartily, and then the Fairy despatched one of her peacocks to her palace to bring a gorgeous robe for Mayblossom, who certainly needed it, for her own was torn to shreds by the thorns and briars. Another peacock was sent to the Admiral to tell him that he could now land in perfect safety, which he at once did, bringing all his men with him, even to Jack-the-Chatterer, who, happening to pass the spit upon which the Admiral's dinner was roasting, snatched it up and brought it with him.

Admiral Cocked-Hat was immensely surprised when he came upon the golden chariot, and still more so to see two lovely

Another Peacock Was Sent to the Admiral

ladies walking under the trees a little farther away. When he reached them, of course he recognized the Princess, and he went down on his knees and kissed her hand quite joyfully. Then she presented him to the Fairy, and told him how Carabosse had been finally routed, and he thanked and congratulated the Fairy, who was most gracious to him.

While they were talking, she cried suddenly: "I declare I smell a savory dinner."

"Why yes, Madam, here it is," said Jack-the-Chatterer, holding up the spit, where all the pheasants and partridges were frizzling. "Will Your Highness please to taste any of them?"

"By all means," said the Fairy, "especially as the Princess will certainly be glad of a good meal."

So the Admiral sent back to his ship for everything that was needful, and they feasted merrily under the trees. By the time they had finished, the peacock had come back with a robe for the Princess, in which the Fairy arrayed her. It was of green and gold brocade, embroidered with pearls and rubies, and her long golden hair was tied back with strings of diamonds and emeralds, and crowned with flowers.

The Fairy made her mount beside her in the golden chariot, and took her on board the Admiral's ship, where she bade her farewell, sending many messages of friendship to the Queen, and bidding the Princess tell her that she was the fifth Fairy who had attended the christening. Then salutes were fired, the fleet weighed anchor, and very soon they reached the port.

Here the King and Queen were waiting, and they received Mayblossom with such joy and kindness that she could not get a word in edgewise, to say how sorry she was for having run away with such a very poor spirited ambassador. But, after all, it must have been all Carabosse's fault.

Just at this lucky moment who should arrive but King Merlin's son, who had become uneasy at not receiving any news from his ambassador, and so had started out himself with a magnificent escort of a thousand horsemen, and thirty body-guards in gold and scarlet uniforms, to see what could have happened.

As he was a hundred times handsomer and braver than the ambassador, the Princess found she could like him very much. So the wedding was held at once, with so much splendor and rejoicing that all the previous misfortunes were quite forgotten.

"May I Have a Bit of Bread?"

THE GOLDEN GOOSE

Once upon a time there was a man who had three sons. The youngest one they called the simpleton, and paid no attention to him at all unless indeed it was to laugh at him.

One day, the eldest son decided to go into the forest to cut some wood. Before he left, his mother prepared for him a loaf of bread and a flask of wine so that he might have neither hunger nor thirst.

Deep into the forest he met a little old man. "Good day to you, kind sir," said the man. "May I have a bit of the bread and wine you carry? I am very hungry and thirsty."

"If I give you of my loaf and wine, there won't be any for me," the boy answered, "so be on your way."

Leaving the little old man standing there, he went to do his work. But it wasn't long before, felling a tree with his hatchet, he would suffer dearly. The hatchet jumped up, as if of its own accord, and hit him in the arm. He had to stop working and go home for it to be tended to.

On another day, the second son went into the forest, his mother having provided food for him in much the same way as she had for his older brother. For this brother too, the little old man was waiting deep in the wood, once more begging for just a little bit of the bread and wine.

But the second son would have none of it. "Leave off, old man," he said. "If I give to you, so much the less have I for myself."

He went deeper into the forest after he had eaten and selected a tree to begin his work on.

But he was at it for only a few moments, when the hatchet jumped out of his hand and hit him in the leg, leaving him so severely wounded that there was nothing to do but limp home to be cared for.

The Hatchet Jumped Out of His Hand

The next day, the simpleton approached his father. "Let me go into the forest today," he said, "for my brothers have not been able to bring the wood we so sorely need."

"Off with you," scoffed his father. "If your brothers could not accomplish this, how could you, who know nothing of the work, think to do so?"

He begged and begged until his father, just to be rid of him, gave his consent. His mother prepared food and drink, not nearly so good as those she had given his brothers, and off the simpleton went.

He was surprised when he met the little old man in the woods. Concerned only with the wounds they had received and caring nothing for others, his brothers had never mentioned encountering any strangers.

But the simpleton returned the little old man's greeting kindly.

"I see you have some bread and wine," said the little old man. "I myself have neither eaten nor drunk for so many days. I wish that I may partake of your simple meal with you."

"More Than Happy to Share"

"By all means, stranger," said the simpleton. "1 am more than happy to share whatever I have with you."

As they sat down to eat together in a clearing in the woods, the plain bread that the simpleton's mother had sent with him became a rich and delicious cake, and the simple everyday beverage a sparkling wine.

The young man and the old enjoyed their meal. When they had finished, the elder turned to the younger and said, "You have a good heart and a willing nature, my son. Because you have given to me, I am going to give to you. Here is a fine bit of luck for you, my young man: Look to that ancient tree yonder. When 1 am gone, you shall cut it down. At its roots, I promise you, you will find something very worth your while." The little old man tipped his fingers to his hat in salute, and disappeared as smoothly as he had first made himself known.

The simpleton approached the tree and chopped away at it as he had been told. Before long, it fell.

Among the tangled roots, something glittered in the sunlight. The simpleton

Filled with Wonder and Curiosity

stooped down and lifted it up in both his hands.

It was a goose, but a goose with feathers of the very purest gold. The simpleton soothed it and spoke to it and tucked it under his arm. Then he made his way to an inn where he wanted to spend the night.

He was made much of in welcome, not only by the landlord of the place, but by his three daughters as well. When they saw the golden goose, they were filled with curiosity and wonder.

The eldest daughter was seized with an urge to have, if not the goose itself, then at least one of its golden feathers. She waited and watched carefully, and when the simpleton had gone out, she grabbed the goose by one of its wings.

But when she tried to pull her hand away, she could not. She was stuck fast and could not move.

The second sister had wanted a golden feather for herself as well; but as soon as she touched her sister, she was held likewise and could not move.

They Zigged, They Zagged

When the two stricken sisters saw the youngest approach, they yelled out to her. "Stay away, stay away!" they shouted.

But she could see no reason to do so. If her sisters could make claim upon the goose, why not she?

But no sooner had she come close and barely touched with her hand the hem of her sister's sleeve, she found that she was stuck fast to her and could not turn herself loose.

And that was the way they had to stay all night.

In the morning, the simpleton took leave of the inn, his goose again tucked under his arm, and he as unmindful of the three girls hanging onto it as if they didn't at all exist.

As he walked quickly along, they had to run to keep up with him.

To the right, to the left, wherever the simpleton went, the three girls had to follow him. When he zigged, they zigged; when he zagged, they zagged. Down the lanes and up the meadows, through forest and field, tired unto exhaustion, still they must follow him.

To the Man Who Made Her Laugh

They ran along so, until they came to a field where a parson was walking. The parson, seeing the three girls in pursuit of the young man, and understanding nothing of it, was struck with dismay. "For shame, you girls, running after a young fellow in this way!" he shouted. He reached out to stop them, grasping the arm of the third sister, but he stuck fast as well and could not remove himself from the procession.

Across from the field in the churchyard, the sexton saw the parson running after the others, and he began to run, too. "Your reverence, your reverence," he called out as he tried to catch up with them. "Have you forgotten that you have a christening to do very soon?" He caught up with them and caught the parson by the hem of his coat, in order to pull him away. Alas, he found himself stuck as well, and pulled along with the others.

As they went on, they passed two peasants hoeing in the next field. "Help, help!" shouted the sexton. "Come at once and set us free!" They dropped their hoes and ran to do his bidding, but no sooner had they touched him but they were stuck as well, and now there were seven people running along with the simpleton and the golden goose.

Soon they came to the castle of a local King. Now this King was blessed with a daughter, but the daughter herself was cursed with the burden of seriousness, a burden so heavy in her case that in all her life she had never once been known to laugh. The King was so concerned for her happiness that he had promised her hand in marriage to the first man who could cause her to laugh out loud.

Now the simpleton knew nothing of this, but when he passed by the palace with all of the seven who were following him, running, kicking, screaming, shouting, crying out for help, and performing all sorts of other antics to free themselves from their condition, the Princess burst out laughing as if she would never stop. The very peals of her laughter were like bells ringing throughout the little kingdom.

The King was very pleased at this; on the other hand, the idea of his daughter marrying a nobody like a simpleton did not seem quite right to him. Nor did he quite know what to do with the sim pleton's hangers-on. After all, it was one thing for a real King to have a court and retainers of his own, but for a simpleton to be burdened with such a motley crew as this did not seem quite the royal thing.

The King conferred with his ministers, and by and by they came up with a plan. In order to marry the Princess, came the royal proclamation, the simpleton must first produce a man who was able to drink up a cellar full of wine.

The simpleton set down the golden goose, enabling him to free himself of his party of people. Then he took himself back to the woods where he had first met the little old man who had led him to the goose.

At the very place where the simpleton had chopped down the tree, now sat another little old man, this one with a very sad face.

"What ails you, my friend?" the simpleton asked kindly.

"I have a thirst, but such a thirst," replied the man, "that I cannot quench. Not a keg of water, not a cask of wine, not all of heaven's droplets can quench this thirst of mine."

"Ah hah!" said the simpleton. "We are well

Simpleton told the king "I am ready for my bride"

met indeed, my friend." Then he explained to the little old man that he would give him drink by the cellar full, if only he would agree to accompany him.

This the little old man gladly did.

Straight away went they to the King's cellar. The little old man sat himself down on a small three-legged stool and the simpleton rolled vat after vat of wine in front of him.

As the whole royal court watched and wondered, the little old man drank his fill until the cellar was quite empty.

At that, the simpleton clapped his hands, and told the King he was ready for his bride.

The King was more annoyed than ever. It made him wretched that such a man, called the simpleton by everybody, should be entitled to his only daughter.

Once again he conferred with the royal ministers, and once again they came up with a seemingly impossible task for the simpleton: he was now to find a man who could eat a mountain full of bread.

The simpleton put a serious face on the

The Old Man Drank His Fill

matter, but chuckled to himself as he hurried along back to the forest and the spot where the magic had first begun.

There sat a man who wore a barrel around his body in place of a suit of clothes. He pounded the barrel with his fists and tears ran down his face.

"Why are you so unhappy, kind sir?" asked the simpleton.

"Because, because," and the man gulped down a sob or two before he could continue, "because I am so hungry and cannot get enough to eat. Already my wife says I have eaten us out of house and home, and all the shops in my village are closed to me, because I have eaten all their wares. Yet," he went on, "I am still so hungry!"

The simpleton knew that the little old man of the forest was defending him still. "Come along with me, friend," he said, taking the poor unfortunate by the arm, "and I will take you to a kingdom where you will surely find your fill to eat."

Meanwhile, at the castle, all the granaries of the kingdom had been emptied, all the

"Eaten Us Out of House and Home"

bakeries put on triple shift to make the bread for the simpleton's next test.

When he arrived, leading the man in the barrel, all the people of the realm watched in wonder.

The simpleton bade his companion to seat himself at the base of the mountain of bread and commence to chew. As the people watched, open mouthed themselves, the mountain grew smaller and smaller, as the man fed himself happily.

The sun was beginning to set over the distant hills, and still the people stood and watched when suddenly there came a loud snapping sound.

The man had burst the staves of his barrel-suit, and the mountain of bread had completely disappeared.

The entire populace cheered and stamped their approval; people like a good show, and no one had ever entertained them quite so much as the simpleton had. They were more than happy to have him as the heir to the throne and their next King.

The Mountain of Bread Completely Disappeared

But the present royal majesty was having none of it. He set yet a third impossible task for the simpleton: now he must find a ship that could sail on land as well as it did on water.

Once more the simpleton went back to the place in the forest.

This time, there sat the little old man with whom he had first shared his simple meal of bread and beverage. The little man smiled at him. "I know why you are here," said he. "Because you were so kind to me when others wouldn't be, I have been pleased to help you," he said, "and now I am ready to help you again, and indeed to be with you in your moment of triumph."

With the very flick of his fingers, the little old man produced the strangest-looking contraption the simpleton had ever seen in his life. It had sticks and sails and wheels and keels and dozens of other devices going every which way; most importantly, as the little old man quickly demonstrated, it could indeed propel itself on land or water.

Soon they were making their merry way down the road toward the King's castle. When

With the Very Flick of His Fingers

they pulled up, as you may be sure, the entire countryside emptied out to meet them.

The little old man stood at the helm, while the simpleton merely folded his arms across his chest, planted his legs firmly on the deck, and smiled out at the gaping crowd.

Soon enough, the little old man had the strange ship doing all wonder of things: it skimmed along the lake in front of the castle and then did a whirligig that brought it sailing up to the very tallest tower. Then off it went up a hill, rolling down again, splashing into the lake and stopping at last on dry land at the very feet of the King himself

At the sight the Princess laughed more merrily than ever, the King withdrew his objections and the Princess laughed again. She gave her hand to the simpleton, and for all we know, she may be laughing still.

She Cut Off a Shining Tress

DORANI

Once upon a time there lived a seller of scents and essences, who had a very beautiful daughter named Dorani. This maiden had a friend who was a fairy, and the two were high in favor with Indra, the ruler of fairyland, because they were able to sing so sweetly and dance so deftly that no one in the kingdom could equal them for grace and beauty.

Dorani had the most lovely hair in the world, for it was like spun gold, and the smell of it was like the smell of fresh roses. But her locks were so long and thick that the weight of it was often unbearable, and one day she cut off a shining tress, and wrapping it in a large leaf, threw it in the river which ran just below her window.

Now it happened that the King's son was out hunting, and had gone down to the river

"Unless I Win That Maiden, I Die!"

to drink, when there floated towards him a folded leaf, from which came a perfume of roses. The Prince, with idle curiosity, took a step into the water and caught the leaf as it was sailing by. He opened it, and within he found a lock of hair like spun gold, from which came a faint, exquisite odor.

When the Prince reached home that day he looked so sad and was so quiet that his father wondered if any ill had befallen him, and asked what was the matter.

Then the youth took from his breast the tress of hair which he had found in the river, and holding it up to the light, replied: "See, my father, was ever hair like this? Unless I may win and marry the maiden that owns that lock I must die!"

So the King immediately sent heralds throughout all his dominions to search for the damsel with hair like spun gold, and at last he learned that she was the daughter of the scent-seller. The object of the herald's mission was quickly told abroad, and Dorani heard it with the rest; and, one day, she said to her father:

"If the hair is mine, and the King requires

The Wedding was Celebrated with Great Rejoicing

me to marry his son, I must do so; but, remember, you must tell him that if, after the wedding, I stay all day at the palace, every night will be spent in my old home."

The old man listened to her with amazement, but answered nothing, as he knew she was wiser than he. Of course the hair was Dorani's, and the heralds soon returned and informed the King, their master, who summoned the scent-seller, and told him that he wished for his daughter to be given in marriage to the Prince.

The father bowed his head three times, and replied: "Your highness is our lord, and all that you bid us we will do. The maiden asks this only – that if, after the wedding, she stays all day at the palace, she may go back each night to her father's house."

The King thought this a very strange request; but said to himself it was, after all, his son's affair, and the girl would surely soon get tired of going to and fro. So he made no difficulty, and everything was speedily arranged and the wedding was celebrated with great rejoicing.

At first, the condition attached to his

"Day After Day She Sits as Though Turned to Stone"

wedding with the lovely Dorani troubled the Prince very little, for he thought that he would at least see his bride all day. But, to his dismay, he found that she would do nothing but sit the whole time upon a stool with her head bowed forward upon her knees, and he could never persuade her to say a single word.

Each evening she was carried in a palanquin to her father's house, and each morning she was brought back soon after daybreak; and yet never a sound passed her lips, nor did she show by any sign that she saw, or heard, or heeded her husband.

One evening the Prince, very unhappy and troubled, was wandering in an old and beautiful garden near the palace. The gardener was a very aged man, who had served the Prince's greatgrandfather, and when he saw the Prince he came and bowed to him, and said:

"Child! Child! Why do you look so sad – what is the matter?"

The Prince replied: "I am sad, old friend, because I have married a wife as lovely as the stars, but she will not speak to me, and I

The Gardner was a aged man

know not what to do. Night after night she leaves me for her father's house, and day after day she sits in mine as though turned to stone, and utters no word, whatever I may do or say."

The old man stood thinking for a moment, and then he hobbled off to his own cottage. A little later he came back to the Prince with five or six small packets, which he placed in his hands and said:.,

"Tomorrow, when your bride leaves the palace, sprinkle the powder from one of these packets upon your body, and while seeing clearly, you yourself will become invisible. More I cannot do for you, but may all go well!"

And the Prince thanked him, and put the packets carefully away.

The next night, when Dorani left for her father's house in her palanquin, the Prince took out a packet of the magic powder and sprinkled it over himself, and then hurried after her. He soon found that, as the old man had promised, he was invisible to everyone, although he felt as usual, and could see all that passed. He speedily overtook the

"Fly, Stool, to the Palace of King Indra"

palanquin and walked beside it to the scent-seller's dwelling. There it was set down, and, when his bride, closely veiled, left it and entered the house, he, too, entered unperceived.

At the first door Dorani removed one veil; then she entered another doorway at the end of a passage where she removed another veil; next she mounted the stairs, and at the door of the women's quarters removed a third veil. After this she proceeded to her own room where were set two large basins, one of attar of roses and one of water; in these she washed herself, and afterwards called for food. A servant brought her a bowl of curds, which she ate hastily, and then arrayed herself in a robe of silver, and wound about her strings of pearls, while a wreath of roses crowned her hair.

When fully dressed, she seated herself upon a four-legged stool over which was a canopy with silken curtains; these she drew around her, and then called out:

"Fly, stool, to the palace of King Indra."

Instantly the stool rose in the air, and the

The Women Sang and Danced

invisible Prince, who had watched all these proceedings with great wonder, seized it by one leg as it flew away, and found himself being borne through the air at a rapid rate.

In a short while they arrived at the house of the fairy who, as mentioned before, was the favorite friend of Dorani. The fairy stood waiting on the threshold, as beautifully dressed as Dorani herself was, and when the stool stopped at her door she cried in astonishment:

"Why, the stool is flying all crooked to-day! What is the reason of that, I wonder? I suspect that you have been talking to your husband, and so it will not fly straight."

But Dorani declared that she had not spoken one word to him, and she couldn't think why the stool flew as if weighed down at one side. The fairy still looked doubtful, but made no answer, and took her seat beside Dorani, the Prince again holding tightly to one leg. Then the stool flew on through the air until it came to the palace of Indra.

All through the night the women sang and danced before the King Indra, whilst a magic lute played of itself the most bewitching

Her Head Bowed Upon Her Knees

music; till the Prince, who sat watching it all, was quite entranced. Just before dawn the King gave the signal to cease; and again the two women seated themselves on the stool, and, with the Prince clinging to the leg, it flew back to earth, and bore Dorani and her husband safely to the scent-seller's shop.

Here the Prince hurried away by himself past Dorani's palanquin with its sleepy bearers, straight on to the palace; and as he passed the threshold of his own rooms he became visible again. Then he awaited Dorani's arrival.

As soon as she arrived, she took a seat and remained as silent as usual, with her head bowed on her knees. For a while not a sound was heard, but presently the Prince said:

"I dreamed a curious dream last night, and as it was all about you I am going to tell it you, although you heed nothing."

The girl, indeed, took no notice of his words, but in spite of that he proceeded to relate every single thing that had happened the evening before, leaving out no detail of all that he had seen or heard.

"Give Me the Magic Lute"

not going to your house, Dorani?" At that she rose and threw herself weeping into his arms, whispering gently:

"Never again, my lord, never again would I leave thee!" So the Prince won his beautiful bride; and though neither of them dealt any further with fairies and their magic, they learnt more daily of the magic of love, which one may still learn, although fairy magic has fled away.

And when he praised her singing – and his voice shook a little – Dorani just looked at him; but she said naught, though, in her own mind, she was filled with wonder. "What a dream!" she thought. "Could it have been a dream? How could he have learnt in a dream all I did and said?" Still she kept silent; she only looked that once at the Prince, and then remained all day as before, with her head bowed upon her knees.

When night came the Prince again made himself invisible and followed her. The same things happened again as had happened before, but Dorani sang better than ever. In the morning the Prince a second time told Dorani all that she had done, pretending that he had dreamt of it. Directly after he finished, Dorani gazed at him, and said:

"Is it true that you dreamt this, or were you really there?"

"I was there," answered the Prince.

"But why do you follow me?" asked Dorani.

"Because," replied the Prince, "I love you, and to be with you is happiness."

This time Dorani's eyelids quivered, but she said no more, and was silent the rest of the day. However, in the evening, just as she was stepping into her palanquin, she said to the Prince: "If you love me, prove it by not following me tonight."

And so the Prince did as she wished, and stayed at home.

That evening the magic stool flew so unsteadily that they could hardly keep their seats, and at last the fairy exclaimed:

"There is only one reason that it should jerk like this! You have been talking to your husband!"

And Dorani replied: "Yes, I have spoken; oh, yes, I have spoken!" But no more would she say.

That night Dorani sang so marvelously that at the end the King Indra rose up and vowed that she might ask what she would and he would give it to her. At first she was silent; but, when he pressed her, she answered: "Give me the magic lute."

The King, when he heard this, was displeased with himself for having made so rash a promise, because this lute he valued above all his possessions. But as he had promised, so he must perform, and with an ill grace he handed it to her.

"You must never come here again," said he, "for, once having asked so much, how will you in future be content with smaller gifts?"

Dorani bowed her head silently as she took the lute, and passed with the fairy out of the great gate, where the stool awaited them. More unsteadily than before, it flew back to earth.

When Dorani got to the palace that morning she asked the Prince whether he had dreamt again. He laughed with happiness, for this time she had spoken to him of her own free will; and he replied:

"No; but I begin to dream now — not of what *has* happened in the past, but of what *may* happen in the future."

That day Dorani sat very quietly, but she answered the Prince when he spoke to her; when evening fell, and with it the time for her departure, she still sat on. Then the Prince came close to her and said softly: "Are you

"Never Again Would I Leave Thee!"